THE SEA SERPENT'S DAUGHTER

For Dawn—who brings new light
into our lives every day.

Library of Congress Cataloging-in-Publication Data

Lippert, Margaret H.
    The sea serpent's daughter: a Brazilian legend / written and
adapted by Margaret H. Lippert; illustrated by Felipe Davalos.
        p.   cm.—(Legends of the world)
    Summary: Relates the traditional Brazilian legend of how the Sea
Serpent's gift of darkness to his daughter brings night to the
people of the rain forest.
    ISBN 0-8167-3053-9 (lib. bdg.)   ISBN 0-8167-3054-7 (pbk.)
    [1. Folklore—Brazil.]   I. Davalos, Felipe, ill.   II. Title.
III. Series.
    PZ8.1.L67Se   1993
    398.21—dc20   92-21438

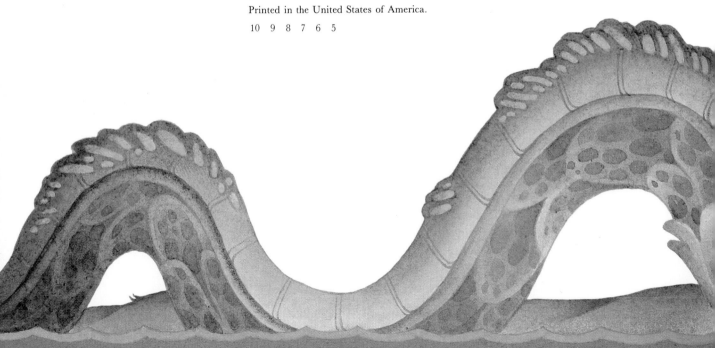

LEGENDS OF THE WORLD

THE SEA SERPENT'S DAUGHTER

A BRAZILIAN LEGEND

WRITTEN AND ADAPTED BY MARGARET H. LIPPERT   ILLUSTRATED BY FELIPE DAVALOS

TROLL ASSOCIATES

Long ago, there was no night. It was daylight all the time. There was no darkness, nor starlight. There was no sunrise, nor sunset. There were no night birds, nor night beasts, nor night insects.

In those long ago days there lived a Great Sea Serpent who was king of the sea. With his daughter, Bonita, he dwelt in a palace made of coral and draped with shining pearls. It was dark and peaceful in the depths of the sea. Whales sang their sweet songs, as sea creatures danced in and out of the shadows. The Great Sea Serpent and his beautiful daughter lived happily at the mouth of the mighty Amazon, where the great river meets the sea.

One day Bonita ventured up to the surface of the water. Soft sand beaches called her to their shores. She emerged from the sea for the very first time. Gentle winds blew against her skin. The sweet smell of fruit beckoned her toward arching tree branches. Wondering at the strange beauty of the land, she strayed farther and farther away from her home and into the dense, green jungle.

At last she came upon a village. People gathered around her. Never before had they seen such a wondrous stranger. Her green eyes sparkled like the sun on the sea. Shining waves of hair flowed down her back.

The chief came forward, taken with her beauty. "Where do you come from?" he asked.

"I come from beneath the sea," she replied. "My father is the Great Sea Serpent, king of the sea."

Bonita's gentle modesty shone through her soft green eyes. The chief fell in love with her at once.

"You are welcome to stay here with us," he said. "Anything you wish need only be asked for, and it shall be granted."

Bonita accepted the chief's kind invitation. Soon, they became good friends. They spoke often of the wonders of their worlds — she, of her life under the sea, and he, of his life on land. In time, they were married and lived happily among their villagers.

After some time had passed, the chief noticed that Bonita looked sad. Day after day she grew more and more weary. At last, the chief asked what he might do to help his wife.

"Oh, my husband," she sighed. "How I miss the darkness of my father's kingdom! Here, it is always light. Though I love the light of your world, I grow tired and wish to rest my eyes."

The chief, in turn, wished for nothing more than the happiness of his wife. Swiftly, he dispatched his three most trusted servants to the kingdom of the Great Sea Serpent. "You must ask him to send some darkness from the depths of the sea," the chief told his men. "Without it, I fear my beloved wife may die in the unending light of our land."

The servants set out on their long, hard journey. At last, they came to the place where the river meets the sea. They walked down the sandy beach and called out their request to the Great Sea Serpent.

Then, they watched the surface of the sea, and waited.

Far away, at the bottom of the ocean, the Great Sea Serpent heard their cry. He made a strong bag out of seaweed. Then, he took some darkness from the depths of the sea and placed it in the bag. He took just enough so that there would be darkness and light every day. And he left just enough so that there would always be darkness at the bottom of the sea.

When he had placed just the right amount of darkness into the bag, he tied it with strong strands of seaweed. Then, he shot up to the surface of the sea, his long tail wound tightly around the bag. The servants watched in terror as he lifted himself above the waves and flung the bag onto the shore.

"There is the darkness for my daughter," he thundered. "Take it to her. Do not open the bag, unless you are in her presence, or great harm will come to you." Then, he leapt into a giant whirlpool.

The servants shook with fear. They dragged the bag to the edge of the jungle. There, they began the long trip back to their village.

At first, all went well. Each man took his turn carrying the load of darkness upon his head. But soon, strange sounds came from within the bag.

Squealing, screeching, humming sounds. Never before had the men heard such sounds. They grew more and more afraid.

"Darkness is a powerful force," said the first man. "Let us leave the bag here and run away!"

"No!" cried the second. "We must give it to the chief. Let us sit on the bag and squash darkness. Maybe then it will be quiet, and we can take it back to our village without more trouble."

The third servant was curious. "I wonder what darkness looks like," he said to the others. "I shall open the bag and see for myself."

"No! No! We will die!" cried the others. But it was too late. The servant had loosened the seaweed ties.

From out of the bag rushed a great black cloud of darkness. For the first time, night fell upon the land. And with night came all the night creatures. Squalling night beasts, screeching night birds, and humming night insects flew out into the darkness. Where night went, its creatures followed. The servants rushed headlong into the jungle, more frightened than ever before!

As darkness covered the land, Bonita looked up into the sky. "Night has come!" she cried. "At last, it is night!" Then, she closed her eyes and slept peacefully.

When she awoke, the first sound she heard was the singing of the birds. "How beautiful the fresh new light is," she said. "And what happy songs the birds sing to welcome the new day!"

From that time on, it has always been so. The birds are the first to awaken and welcome the *madrugada*, the early morning, with their beautiful songs.

When daylight came, the three servants crept home with their empty bag.

"Why did night come before you arrived?" the chief asked them. The servants had to admit they had opened the bag, defying the Great Sea Serpent. They had not waited to bring the gift of night to his daughter.

"For your act of disobedience, I shall change you into monkeys," the chief cried. "From this time forth, you shall live in the trees." At once, the three servants turned into chattering monkeys.

Bonita picked up the empty bag and looked inside. At the bottom of the bag lay a glistening oyster shell. "I shall send this to the sky," Bonita said, "so that people everywhere will always remember my father and his generous gift of darkness."

She threw the shell high into the sky, where it became the moon. A handful of glittering sand marked its path and became the stars.

Now we have darkness and light every day. Between the darkness and light we have dawn, heralded by a chorus of singing birds. As the darkness descends we have dusk, when night birds, night beasts, and night insects awaken.

And always we remember the gentle Bonita and her loving father, the king of the sea, who made it so.

People from many cultures have different stories to explain the origin of night. *The Sea Serpent's Daughter* is a Brazilian legend about how night came to the people of the rain forest. Such stories, or myths, of how something came to be are known in Spanish as *ejemplos,* or *leyendas*.

The Amazon River Basin, where the story takes place, makes up the world's largest tropical rain forest. The region has a great variety of animals. More than 1,500 kinds of birds, including toucans, macaws, parakeets, and parrots, live in the rain forest. Chattering monkeys, like the ones in the story, can be seen jumping from tree to tree. Anacondas, boa constrictors, anteaters, and all sorts of insects can also be found in this region.

Few people live in the rain forest, however, because of the harsh land and climate. The rainfall averages between 50 and 120 inches (127 and 305 centimeters) a year. Trees as tall as 200 feet (61 meters) grow so close together that little sunlight ever reaches the ground.

The region is a source of lumber and rubber for people the world over. Preservation of the land has also become a source of great interest as people become aware of the important role rain forests play in keeping our earth a healthy and balanced place to live.

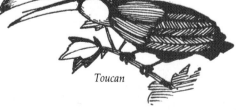
Toucan

32